CARS
GALORE

Peter Stein

illustrated by Bob Staake

WALKER BOOKS
AND SUBSIDIARIES
LONDON • BOSTON • SYDNEY • AUCKLAND

Black car, green car,
nice car, mean car.
Near car, far car.
Whoa! Bizarre car!

Fast car, slow car,
on-the-go car.
Big car, small car.
Has-it-all car.

Cars and MORE cars!
Doing-chores cars!
Rev-'em-up-and-
make-'em-ROAR cars!

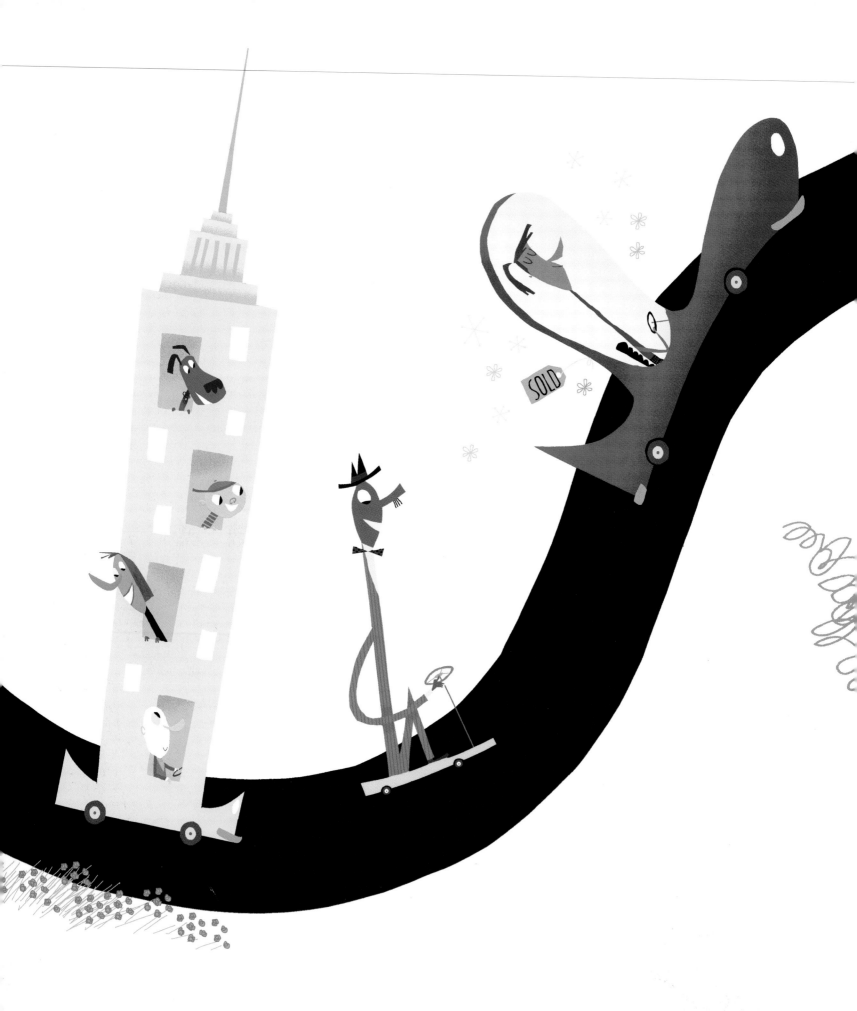

Tall car, short car,
fun-filled fort car.
New car, old car.
Has-a-cold car!

Jazz car, soul car,
rock 'n' roll car.
Blues car, song car.
Sing-along car!

Cars on highways!
Cars on cliffs!
Cars on skyways!
Cars on lifts!

Hundred-feet car.
Incomplete car.
Scary shark car.
Noah's Ark car!

Plug-in motors.
Solar motors.
Igloo ice-fuelled
polar motors!

Eco-friendly,
runs-on-air car!
Zzzip-around-
without-a-care car!

Cars and cars and
yet still MORE cars!
Millions, billions,
cars-GALORE cars!

Honk cars! *BEEP* cars!
At-a-creep cars!
Miles of piles of
in-a-heap cars!

Cars off-roading,
jumping, thumping!
Gears all grinding!
Pistons pumping!

Cars for racing!
Cars with might!
Cars for chasing!
Hold on tight!

Rusty, dusty,
hunk-of-junk car.
Stinky, yucky,
smells-like-a-skunk car.

Save it! Tow it!
Big repair job!
Have-a-bath-and-
rinse-with-care job!

Quick drive, ICK drive!
Makes-you-sick drive!
Round-and-round drive!
Upside-down drive!

But **shhh...**

This car's snoozing.
That car's snoring.
Done with cruising.
Truly boring.

Pack-it-up-and-
take-a-trip car!
Crank-it-up-and-
let-'er-rip car!

Fun drive, sun drive,
Got-to-run drive!
Dream drive, cool drive...

One day
YOU'LL
drive!

To Gabriel and Elias,
my favourite back-seat drivers
P. S.

For Nicole and Kelli
B. S.

First published 2011 by Walker Books Ltd
87 Vauxhall Walk, London SE11 5HJ

This edition published 2013

2 4 6 8 10 9 7 5 3 1